**Title**

**Growing In Christ Through The Book Of James:
12 Bible Studies**

By Rick Gillespie-Mobley

## Dedication Page

To My Wife Toby Lynne Gillespie-Mobley Who

Has Listened To Me Preach For Over 34 Years

And Continues To Pray For Me

To The People Of Roxbury Presbyterian Church,

Glenville New Life Community Church, New Life

Fellowship, Calvary Presbyterian Church & New

Life At Calvary Who Came Sunday After Sunday

To Hear Me Teach Bible Studies And Preached

To The People Of Greater Cleveland Who

Listened To  Our Radio Broadcasts And Watched

Us On TV During The Past 20 Years

To The Lay Pastors  & Teachers, Helen Britt,

Sylvia Fields, Walter Glenn, Katy Glenn, Gerald

Nevins, Felicia Earl, Denise Nevins, Jeanette

Williams-Daniels, Jameel Williams-Daniels,

LaVerne Wilcox, Andrea Billups, LaTanya Deane,

Pastor Toby and Pastor Kellie Who Made These

Lessons Come Alive In Small Groups

To All Those Who Journeyed Through The

Lessons In Life-Sharing.

To God For The Gifts He Gives To Me To Pass To

Others

## Overview:

The twelve bible study lessons follow the outline breakup commonly found in the NIV bible. The lesson topics are 1) Victorious In Trials, 2) Battling Back Temptation, 3) True Religion: More Than Just Talk—Listen Then Do, 4) Getting A Grip On Prejudice And Discrimination, 5) Going Further Than The Demons, 6) Grabbing Hold Of Your Tongue, 7) Two Kinds Of Wisdom, 8) Submit To God And Find What You Need, 9) Boasting About Tomorrow, 10) Bad Employers And Getting Rich, 11) Patience In Suffering, and 12) The Power Of The Prayer Of Faith

These twelve bible studies are designed for small group discussion groups, yet they can also be used by individuals in their own personal growth. The bible studies have been designed with three specific purposes. The first purpose is to get the participants to study the word of God and learn what it actually teaches. There are so many things today that people think are in the bible, that are not there in the actual texts of Scripture. The second purpose is to apply the texts of Scriptures to the participants' live so that a life transformation process can take place. The Holy Spirit can work more effectively in open hearts. The third purpose is to build positive relationships among the participants. People can learn from each other because God is at work in all of our lives but at different stages and levels.

### Life-Sharing Lesson 1  James 1:1-12
### "Victorious In Trials"

Most likely, you've heard the age-old question, "If God is good, how can He let bad things happen?" Since the fall of man, life has always included hardship. Though trials are painful, understanding the Lord's purpose can bring joy and hope.

The Word of God is clear that suffering is purposeful. Primarily, the Lord is conforming His children to be like Jesus (2 Cor. 3:18). When a person is newly saved, he or she still has many "rough edges." Sanctification, which takes place from that point on, is the process of becoming holy—and few things build character like sorrow. Unfortunately, people rarely mature during pleasant times. Instead, pain brings impurities to the surface and forces people to see the reality of their life.

Another reason the Father allows trials is to test the faith of His children. Of course, He doesn't need this for His own information—it is the believers who benefit. Tested faith is stronger and more reliable than untried faith.

Furthermore, God allows hardship in order to reveal His character, love, and power. During life's storms, people who cling to their heavenly Father will find Him trustworthy and real. When the next difficulty arises, they'll remember His faithfulness during the previous trial and will rest confidently in Him.

While no one wants to suffer, experience and sorrow will mature the believer. We can learn certain things from books and other people's stories, but most growth occurs during trials. So, when problems occur and sorrow seems piercing, thank God for His purpose in your suffering. (In Touch Daily Devotional)

1. What was one of the last trials that you faced?

**James 1:1-12 (NIV)**
[1] James, a servant of God and of the Lord Jesus Christ, To the twelve tribes scattered among the nations: Greetings. [2] Consider it pure joy, my brothers and sisters, whenever you face trials of many kinds, [3] because you know that the testing of your faith develops perseverance. [4] Perseverance must finish its work so that you may be mature and complete, not lacking anything. [5] If any of you lacks wisdom, he should ask God, who gives generously to all without finding fault, and it will be given to him. [6] But when the person asks, he must believe and not doubt, because he who doubts is like a wave of the sea, blown and tossed

by the wind. [7] That person should not think he will receive anything from the Lord; [8] he is a double-minded man, unstable in all he does. [9] The brother or sister in humble circumstances ought to take pride in his high position.
[10] But the one who is rich should take pride in his low position, because he will pass away like a wild flower. [11] For the sun rises with scorching heat and withers the plant; its blossom falls and its beauty is destroyed. In the same way, the rich man will fade away even while he goes about his business.
[12] Blessed is the person who perseveres under trial, because when he has stood the test, he will receive the crown of life that God has promised to those who love him.

1a. Which James is writing this letter?

2. What do you think it means for you to be a servant of God?

3. How are believers scattered to day, and what impact does that have on us understanding this book?

4. What is your normal reaction when you face a trial in your life?

5. Do you handle your trials differently depending on the location the trial occurs for example is it different at church than at work or school?

6. Why does James want us to consider it a joy when we face trials?

7. Why do we need perseverance in our faith?

8. If God is good, why do we have to endure suffering?

9. What kind of wisdom do you think James is referring to in verse 5?

10. How can we tell if we believe and at the same time not doubt?

11. What do you think a double-minded person is?

12. How does a proper view of death in Christ put poverty and riches in perspective?

13. What has to happen to actually receive the crown of life?

14. What does it mean to love the Lord?

10. How are God's gifts different than the gifts we can get through sin?

11. What birth is being discussed in verse 18?

12. What is meant by the "word of truth"?

13. Why is it an honor and privilege to be part of the first fruits in verse 18?

14. What should we do when we yield to temptation?

## Life-Sharing Lesson 3  James 1:19-18 "True Religion: More Than Just Talk- Listen Then Do"

1. When was a time you spoke before you knew all the facts and then had to regret you had spoken ?

**James 1:19-27 (TNIV)**
[19] My dear brothers and sisters, take note of this: Everyone should be quick to listen, slow to speak and slow to become angry, [20] because our anger does not produce the righteousness that God desires. [21] Therefore, get rid of all moral filth and the evil that is so prevalent and humbly accept the word planted in you, which can save you.
[22] Do not merely listen to the word, and so deceive yourselves. Do what it says.
[23] Those who listen to the word but do not do what it says are like people who look at their faces in a mirror [24] and, after looking at themselves, go away and immediately forget what they look like. [25] But those who look intently into the perfect law that gives freedom, and continue in it—not forgetting what they have heard, but doing it—they will be blessed in what they do.
[26] Those who consider themselves religious and yet do not keep a tight rein on their tongues

## Life-Sharing Lesson 4 James 2:1-13

## "Getting A Grip On Prejudice & Discrimination"

1. What did you feel inside the last time you were discriminated against by someone?

2. What do you think causes prejudice and discrimination?

3. Suppose you were told, next week a group of people from the suburbs were coming to our church because they were thinking of becoming members. What would you be willing to do to go out of your way to make them feel welcome?

4. Suppose instead of a group from the suburbs, I told you it was a group coming from the

downtown homeless shelter, would your feelings and emotions be exactly the same? Why?

5. God often sends people to our church that are different. On a scale of 1-10 how much do you go out of your way to speak to them and introduce yourself to them.

**James 2:1-13 (TNIV)**
[1] My brothers and sisters, believers in our glorious LORD Jesus Christ must not show favoritism.
[2] Suppose someone comes into your meeting wearing a gold ring and fine clothes, and a poor person in filthy old clothes also comes in. [3] If you show special attention to the one wearing fine clothes and say, "Here's a good seat for you," but say to the one who is poor, "You stand there" or "Sit on the floor by my feet,"
[4] have you not discriminated among yourselves and become judges with evil thoughts? [5] Listen, my dear brothers and sisters: Has not God chosen those who are poor in the eyes of the world to be rich in faith and to inherit the kingdom he promised those who love him?

## Life-Sharing Lesson 5  James 2:14-26 "Going Further Than The Demons"

1. Why do you think most people believe in some kind of a god?

2. What comes to your mind when you hear that a person is "all talk?"

3. Are we saved by faith or by our actions?

## James 2:14-26 (TNIV)

[14] What good is it, my brothers and sisters, if people claim to have faith but have no deeds? Can such faith save them?
[15] Suppose a brother or sister is without clothes and daily food.
[16] If one of you says to them, "Go in peace; keep warm and well fed," but does nothing about their physical needs, what good is it?
[17] In the same way, faith by itself, if it is not accompanied by action, is dead.

[18] But someone will say, "You have faith; I have deeds." Show me your faith without deeds, and I will show you my faith by what I do.
[19] You believe that there is one God. Good! Even the demons believe that—and shudder. [20] You foolish person, do you want evidence that faith without deeds is useless ?
[21] Was not our father Abraham considered righteous for what he did when he offered his son Isaac on the altar? [22] You see that his faith and his actions were working together, and his faith was made complete by what he did.
[23] And the scripture was fulfilled that says, "Abraham believed God, and it was credited to him as righteousness," and he was called God's friend.
[24] You see that people are justified by what they do and not by faith alone.
[25] In the same way, was not even Rahab the prostitute considered righteous for what she did when she gave lodging to the spies and sent them off in a different direction?
[26] As the body without the spirit is dead, so faith without deeds is dead.

4. How do you reconcile James 2:17 with the following verses from Ephesians 2:8-10:

**Ephesians 2:8-10 (TNIV)** [8] For it is by grace you have been saved, through faith—and this is not from yourselves, it is the gift of God— [9] not by

but it makes great boasts. Consider what a great forest is set on fire by a small spark.

[6] The tongue also is a fire, a world of evil among the parts of the body. It corrupts the whole person, sets the whole course of one's life on fire, and is itself set on fire by hell.

[7] All kinds of animals, birds, reptiles and sea creatures are being tamed and have been tamed by human beings,

[8] but no one can tame the tongue. It is a restless evil, full of deadly poison.

[9] With the tongue we praise our LORD and Father, and with it we curse human beings, who have been made in God's likeness.

[10] Out of the same mouth come praise and cursing. My brothers and sisters, this should not be.

[11] Can both fresh water and salt water flow from the same spring?

[12] My brothers and sisters, can a fig tree bear olives, or a grapevine bear figs? Neither can a salt spring produce fresh water.

3. Do you think James is trying to discourage people from actually becoming teachers? Why or Why not?

4. Why is James holding teachers and leaders to a seemingly higher standard than he does others?

5. Do you think James is teaching there are some people who are perfect in verse2?

6. How does controlling one's speech keep the rest of the body in line?

7. How does the use of the tongue affect the life of your church?

8. What type of fires does the tongue start? What are some of the sins you can think of that are related to the tongue?

7. What do you think bitter envy is, and where does it come from?

8. How have you seen selfish ambition manifest itself in your own life? Why are we tempted to deny that it exists?

9. How does selfish ambition manifest itself in the life of a church?

10. Why can it be difficult to detect that our desires are rooted in selfish ambition coming from the evil one and not coming from God as we might think they are?

11. Where is the emphasis being placed on the wisdom that comes from above?

12. How does verse 17 compare with **Philippians 2:3-4 (TNIV)**
[3] Do nothing out of selfish ambition or vain conceit. Rather, in humility value others above yourselves, [4] not looking to your own interests but each of you to the interests of the others.

13. Which trait in verse 17 of the wisdom which comes from above would you like to see manifested more often in your life?

14. What kind of person comes to your mind when you think of peacemakers? Who is a person you view as a peacemaker?

8. How should be go about resisting the devil?

9. What are the steps James gives to us that are necessary for us to draw near to God?

10. How does humbling ourselves before the Lord relate to the way in which we treat each other?

11. What does it mean to slander someone? How are slander and gossip related?

12. When are you most likely to involve yourself in some type of slander?

13. What is James trying to get us to understand with his verses on not judging the law?




14. What's the difference between holding others accountable for their actions and judging them?

## Life-Sharing Lesson 10 James 5:1-6 "Bad Employers & Getting Rich"

1. If you won a million dollars and had to give it all away and not to family, how would you honestly feel about it?

2. How do you know when you have enough in terms of possessions?

## James 5:1-6 (NIV)

[1] Now listen, you rich people, weep and wail because of the misery that is coming upon you. [2] Your wealth has rotted, and moths have eaten your clothes. [3] Your gold and silver are corroded. Their corrosion will testify against you and eat your flesh like fire. You have hoarded wealth in the last days. [4] Look! The wages you failed to pay the workmen who mowed your fields are crying out against you. The cries of the harvesters have reached the ears of the Lord Almighty. [5] You have lived on earth in luxury and self-indulgence. You have fattened yourselves in the day of slaughter. [6] You have condemned and murdered innocent men, who were not opposing you.

3. What is the tone of James 5:1-6? How would you feel if it was a note somebody passed to you about you?

4. What is there to weep and wail about?

5. Why do you think more money leads to more greed?

6. What's the difference between saving and hoarding? How do you know when you have crossed the line?

7. Is there anything you have accumulated that others would look at you and think that may be

land to yield its valuable crop and how patient he is for the autumn and spring rains. .
[8] You too, be patient and stand firm, because the Lord's coming is near. [9] Don't grumble against each other, brothers, or you will be judged. The Judge is standing at the door! [10] Brothers, as an example of patience in the face of suffering, take the prophets who spoke in the name of the Lord. [11] As you know, we consider blessed those who have persevered. You have heard of Job's perseverance and have seen what the Lord finally brought about. The Lord is full of compassion and mercy. [12] Above all, my brothers, do not swear-- not by heaven or by earth or by anything else. Let your "Yes" be yes, and your "No," no, or you will be condemned.

5. What is the tone of this passage above, James 5:7-12?

6. How long is James telling us to be patient in James 5:7? What causes us to want to bring an end to our patience in a situation?

7. What point is James trying to get through to us by using the illustration of a farmer?

8. How should we interpret verse 8 when it says "the Lord's coming is near."

9. What are some areas in society in which you think the Lord is calling the church to stand firm?

10. What causes us to grumble against one another in the church?

11. Do you think we take seriously the Scriptures warning that we will be judged rather harshly for grumbling and complaining? Why or Why not?

8. What is our responsibility when others confess their sins to us?

9. What should you say to a person who says, "I'm going to confess something to you, but first you must promise me you will not tell anybody?

10. Do you think it takes someone kind of special to be able to pray and keep it from raining or is that an option opens to all of us?

11. How important is it for us to reach out to people who have left the faith? How should we go about doing it? How is leaving the church different from leaving the faith?

12. What death is James referring to in verse 20?